RAFFLES

DISCOVERS THE MAGIC

FIRST EDITION

SALLY AND LOWRI SEAGER

ILLUSTRATIONS BY LAYLA COPE

Grosvenor House
Publishing Limited

This book is published by
Grosvenor House Publishing Ltd
Link House
140 The Broadway, Tolworth, Surrey, KT6 7HT.
www.grosvenorhousepublishing.co.uk

A CIP record for this book
is available from the British Library

ISBN 978-1-83975-720-4

eBook ISBN 978-1-83975-721-1

Preface

Raffles is a happy, friendly, inquisitive and adventurous springer spaniel. He is always ready to give you a tail-wag and a quick spin.

If Raffles could choose another animal to be best friends with, it would most certainly be someone equally affectionate and energetic – that's where we discovered an equally adventurous and agile monkey.

But a youthful duo might need a steadying influence, someone with experience and knowledge that might not be valued in today's hectic world, so we found Grandpa George.

We have been lucky enough to travel and live in Asian countries and were inspired by their vibrancy, colour and friendliness: it seemed right to put our

'Three Adventurers' in one of those settings.

We hope you enjoy this book as much as we have enjoyed writing it. Watch out for our trio's next adventure coming soon – in Egypt!

* * * * *

We are delighted to have worked with Layla Cope, whose amazing work can be seen **@laylas.murals** on Instagram, and Jane Read, our copyeditor and proof-reader.

Follow Raffles **@bemoreraffles** on Instagram for news, photos and videos (including creative videos produced by both authors with Raffles as the main star, of course).

Sally and Lowri Seager

If adventure and love is what you require,
with a sprinkle of dust, you will
get your desire.
Into the future or back in the past,
All these adventures could
have you aghast,
But care for me as your best friend
For if I break the magic will end.

Contents

1

Not the Usual
Monday Morning

The sounds increased and the pounding on the stairs grew louder as Raffles sprang out of bed. After a quick shake, he pressed his soft wet nose against the bottom of the kitchen door, making sniffling, whiffling noises.

The door flew open and Florence rushed in, delighted at the greeting Raffles gave her. His tail really was the waggiest she had ever seen.

'Oh Raffles, how lucky we are to have such a wonderful dog, I love you so much. I do hope you will be OK with Grandpa today,' said Florence, looking concerned. But the springer spaniel was too busy chasing his tail in excitement to take any notice of what Florence had just said.

Jack, Florence's older brother, bounded into the kitchen and threw himself into Raffles's bed. Raffles joined him and it was difficult to see how they could untangle themselves.

'It's my turn to cuddle him now,' said Florence hopefully.

Raffles just loved all the fuss. This was his special family and every day was better than the last. More fun. More cuddles. More walks. The children adored him, and since Freddie, the new baby, had joined the family, Raffles had enjoyed long days at home with lots of company.

Unknown to Raffles, however, today was going to reveal a whole new world to him.

Mum appeared in the kitchen doorway, holding baby Freddie. This particular morning her hair was tied back in a pink ribbon, her make-up was bright and she looked ready to go out. This was not at all like other mornings when she came downstairs with a tangle of hair tumbling onto her shoulders and toothpaste splodges on her T-shirt. Today, Mrs Eva Watson was starting back to work!

After a hurried breakfast, Jack and Florence gave Raffles two sloppy kisses and a quick ear-rub, leaving bits of toast and cereal in his fur. Picking up packed lunches and school bags they scurried out of the house with Dad.

'Come on, Raffles. You are coming with me today,' said Mum, putting on his multi-coloured lead. 'We are taking you to stay with Grandpa for the day. I know he is a little grumpy and sad but I am sure he will love having you there to keep him company.'

For the last few years, Grandpa George had been living on his own. Grandma, his lifelong companion and only true love, had passed away. She had been the life and soul of his existence, and had brought such fun and laughter to all of the Watson family. He missed her dreadfully.

The long days since Grandma's death had stretched out and, over time, Grandpa had gradually become quieter and sadder. Every effort to brighten his days had been useless, as he sat alone in the bay window of his antique shop, deep in thought. The antique shop was where he and Grandma had spent many years together, but no one called there these days and the place had become run-down and dusty.

Mum collected all of Freddie's things into a blue changing bag and wrapped the baby like a cocoon in his outdoor clothes. Another small bag contained some dog food and treats, which Raffles could smell. He let out an enthusiastic bark.

This was exciting. Going out so early in the morning for a walk was Raffles's idea of bliss. With his tail in the air and his nose to the floor he headed quickly out of the door with Mum at the end of the lead.

'You mustn't pull like that, Raffles. We have to walk down the High Street and I need to call in at the butcher's on the way, so you need to stay close.' Raffles's ears pricked up when he heard the butcher mentioned and the thought of juicy sausages and sizzling burgers floated around his head as he licked his lips.

Bruno, the boxer dog from across the road, was out walking too. A little bark from both of them spread some morning cheer across the neighbourhood.

In no time at all they were outside Bertie's butchery shop. Mum called in to say hello. 'Sorry I can't stop, as I'm back to work today. Any chance of picking up a string of sausages on my way back at four o'clock this afternoon?' she asked.

'No problem at all, Mrs Watson. I'll have them ready for you.' Bertie waved and made a funny face at Freddie. Freddie chuckled and Raffles licked his lips.

At the end of the road, just as the church bells chimed eight o'clock, they arrived at Grandpa's antique shop. The old wooden door was pushed open and a small bell rang out, alerting the owner that they had entered.

'Hello, Dad. It's only us,' called Mum. 'I'm just dropping Raffles off with you. I do hope you'll be able to take good care of him and that he isn't too difficult for you to manage.'

From the back of the shop appeared a small and slightly stooped figure, walking slowly down the corridor. He had a sprinkling of tufty white hair on his head and a small neat moustache. Half-moon glasses were balanced on the tip of his nose, framing bright blue eyes. He wore a soft white shirt with a hand-knitted pullover. As Grandpa shuffled towards them smiling, his eyes revealed a sadness that Raffles had not noticed before.

Raffles leapt forwards with excitement, nearly knocking Grandpa down in the process.

'Whoa, boy! Slowly! I'm not as steady on my two feet as you are on your four,' Grandpa exclaimed, keeping a tight grip on his walking stick.

'I'm sure Raffles and I will get on just fine, Eva. I have some nice biscuits we can share for elevenses. You get off to work and don't worry about us. Enjoy your day. I will expect you back around four o'clock.' Grandpa smiled at Eva and Freddie.

'Absolutely, call me if you need anything,' replied a rather anxious-looking Mum as she left the shop hurriedly. 'Love you both. Be good. Byeee!'

With a jingle of the doorbell, she and Freddie left the shop and everything fell quiet.

2

Raffles's Discovery

Grandpa sat down with a rather big thump onto his rocking chair, which let out a grumbling creak. Raffles followed him and sat right next to him, very keen to hear more about the biscuits.

There was a large wooden chest beside Grandpa, covered with a tattered and frayed Indian rug. Raffles jumped up onto it and realized that he had a great view of the High Street and all the people walking by. He spent a while watching the comings and goings of people rushing from one shop to another. There were lots of dogs out walking too and Raffles wanted nothing more than to be outside running around like them. That was until the rustle of a biscuit packet filled the air. Surely it wasn't eleven o'clock already!

Crumbly, buttery, oaty biscuits were pulled out of the packet one by one by Grandpa's big fingers and delicately placed into his mouth. Some biscuits were dunked into his hot steamy mug on the way and became extremely soggy in the process. From mug to mouth Raffles watched with full attention, each one making his mouth fill with anticipation. A big fat dribble started to run from his bottom lip, trickling down like a heavy raindrop onto the rug below.

'Oh no! Raffles, stop drooling,' Grandpa said, sitting forwards and reaching for his hanky. 'You want one, do you? Hmmm, go on then. Just the one. These were really meant for later.' Grandpa broke one of the biscuits in half and gently offered one piece to Raffles, who accepted it with much gratitude and a lot of crunching. Sadly, the rest of the biscuits were then put away in a top drawer.

Reaching for the newspaper by his side, Grandpa immersed himself in the daily goings-on of the local town. He brushed a couple of biscuit crumbs that had rested on his pullover onto the floor.

'I'll save those for later,' Raffles thought to himself.

He turned his head to take in more of his surroundings. What a strange place this was. Everything was old and dusty and the funny smell of the shop became overpowering to Raffles's sensitive nose. Everything looked a little dull and boring to him.

Along the width and length of the shop items of furniture were piled up with only narrow walkways between them. Old curtains and materials tumbled to the floor. and ornaments which had once adorned the grandest of houses were stacked on top of boxes; all were covered in a thick layer of dust. Clocks ticked away quietly, while regal-looking people looked down from dark paintings.

Raffles jumped down from the chest and flopped his hairy body onto a beanbag beside Grandpa, who had now drifted off to sleep and was snoring lightly. 'What a boring day this is going to be,' thought Raffles as he kicked out his back legs to get comfortable. His front paws nestled against his wet brown nose as he was enveloped by the soft, billowing bed.

As he lay there, the thought of playing in the garden, rabbits in the field and pheasants on the lawn floated through his mind. Ten long minutes passed with his eyelids becoming heavier and heavier; his long eyelashes fluttered like butterflies landing on a leaf and it became impossible to keep his big brown eyes open.

Suddenly, from the darkest corner of the shop something glistened like a jewel. Raffles sat bolt upright with his nose up in the air and his long kinky ears dangling by his chocolate and white face.

'What on earth was that?' he thought, as he got up from his beanbag.

Nose to the floor and bushy tail wagging, Raffles darted over to the corner of the room where the sparkle had come from. It was an especially dreary and dusty part of the room, filled with objects towering from floor to ceiling. Things that Raffles had never seen before. Things that looked very unloved.

After a few moments of looking for something shiny, making sure he didn't wake Grandpa or knock anything over, Raffles pushed his nose in between two heavy pieces of furniture. He could smell something unusual and was sure this was where the sparkle had come from. With one last push, his nose hit something and with a bit of a struggle he managed to wiggle it out from between the furniture. 'What can it be?' he wondered.

As he pulled out his discovery it started to become clearer.

The figure was a light dusty-brown colour, with what appeared to be two hairy legs, two long arms, two mango-shaped ears, two glistening bright eyes and … a tail!? Raffles looked closer.

A grubby frayed ribbon was wrapped around the middle of the being. At the end of the ribbon hung a small but elaborate brass key. Raffles noticed that just below the ribbon was a fairly large rip where some of the creature's stuffing was poking out.

Was this an animal? Was this a friend? Was it something scary? Raffles didn't know quite what to make of it.

Raffles pressed his nose against it and after a few snuffles and whiffles, he took one large sniff in order to try and work out what it could be. All of a sudden Raffles pulled back his head. What on earth was about to happen to him?

A surge of a million bubbles started rising up into his nose! His eyes started to water and his nose began to tingle uncontrollably.

'Achooo! Achooo! Achooo!', exploded Raffles.

As he opened his eyes a large puff of dust surrounded him. He shut his eyes again and he quickly turned his nose to the floor as another explosion happened.

'Achooo! Achooo! Achooo!', he sneezed again.

As the tickles finally left his nose, Raffles cautiously opened his eyes. The large fog of dust was finally clearing and various outlines and shapes now started to reappear. But wait! These weren't the outlines of the objects in the antique shop!

A hustle and bustle of movement and noise grew louder and louder as the dust cleared.

What Raffles saw next, you wouldn't believe!

3

Strange Places

Bright blues, vibrant yellows, luscious reds and rich greens dazzled Raffles's eyes, as warm rays of sunshine spread across his back.

Exotic aromas and unfamiliar sounds overloaded his senses, making it hard for him to concentrate on what he was now seeing. Big brown cows with rings through their noses were ambling at the side of the road; piles of fruit and vegetables were scattered around market stalls which stretched as far as he could see. Raffles was standing right in the middle of the hustle with small children and adults rushing past him in a frenzy of both excitement and purpose, each one stepping dangerously close to his tail.

'BEEP BEEEEEP!!'

Raffles quickly ran for the nearest cover and cowered under a plastic sheet. Where on earth was he? How did he get here? And most importantly, where was Grandpa?

Alone and uneasy, Raffles tried his best to be brave but he could feel a little whimper creeping up from his belly. He was frightened by all the noises and commotion of this unfamiliar place and didn't know what to do.

Suddenly a small creature jumped in front of him causing him to start. 'Hello Raffles.'

Raffles quickly tilted his head on one side. There before him was a familiar but strange creature, one he felt he had seen before. Standing as tall as a pheasant and as wide as three gravy bones, Raffles could now make out that the creature was indeed a monkey! A hairy monkey! This was the creature from Grandpa's shop!

With his long slender tail propping him up, the monkey had a big smile on his face, whilst his glistening eyes looked at Raffles, waiting for a reply.

'H-h-hello,' Raffles stuttered, realising words were now coming out of his mouth rather than barks. 'Who are you and w-w-where are we?'

'My name's Sunny and you've brought me home,' replied the monkey, grinning even more widely.

'Home?' asked Raffles with confusion.

'Yes, home! This is where I come from and I know why we are here. Quick, follow me, Raffles — we must get there before bedtime.' And with that, the monkey leapt up and ran into the crowds.

With no time to gather his thoughts or ask any further questions, Raffles was forced to follow Sunny. He definitely didn't want to be left on his own in this new and scary place.

4

A Bumpy Journey

Over and under stalls, in and out of traffic, through and by rivers they ran. Leaping in between sandalled feet and clambering up stone walls, Raffles could feel himself getting hotter and hotter.

His urgency to keep up with the monkey grew as it dawned on him how far away from home he now was. He recognized nothing.

Grabbing a slurp of water from a river on the way, they piled onto the back of a tuk-tuk which was apparently heading in the direction they needed. It was a funny-looking local taxi covered in beads and flowers.

Just as Raffles started to get his breath back and was about to ask Sunny some important questions, the monkey bounded off the back of the tuk-tuk and ran onto the platform of a jam-packed train station. Raffles followed him, squeezing between people's legs and trying his best to keep an eye on the furry figure. Raffles knew that the monkey was the only hope he had of getting back to Grandpa.

As they boarded the train by the nearest carriage, Raffles caught up with Sunny and collapsed in a heap next to him, panting like a steam engine. Raffles caught a glimpse of himself in the reflection of the metal carriage side and saw that he looked more like a grizzly bear than a dog. The humidity and the running had made his ears go even kinkier and his long pink tongue hung out of his mouth as he panted to get cool.

'Please tell me where we are and what we are doing here,' Raffles gasped to Sunny, who was now trying to push his stuffing back into the hole in his tummy.

'I'm sorry, Raffles, now we are on the train I can start to explain. I am Sunny. I am from here, India …'

'INDIA!' yelled Raffles, feeling even more sweaty and perplexed. This was a place Raffles had only heard of and seen on the TV when Mr Watson watched his travel documentaries.

'Yes, India,' Sunny continued, placing a friendly hand on Raffles's ear. 'I was made here a long time ago and was owned by a little girl called Tamira; a beautiful little girl, my friend. I used to live with her in the most wonderful place. We used to spend all our time laughing, playing and having the best of times. I used to be loved, you know, and I used to look so smart,' he said, looking down at his torn tummy and frayed ribbon.

Puzzled, Raffles replied with concern, 'What happened to you?'

'I am old,' said the monkey, 'I have been on many adventures in my life and have the marks to show for it.' He gulped. It was evident he was filled with memories.

'But how did we get here, why are we here and where are we going?' Questions continued to tumble out of Raffles's mouth.

'All will become clear, Raffles, try not to worry. This is our stop, follow me.' And with that, Sunny and Raffles jumped off the train and onto a different platform.

Raffles was starting to get hungry now and his tummy rumbled loudly. As if the rumble had requested it, a small piece of meat was flung towards him by the monkey, who had helped himself from a food stall. Sunny was so fast that even the stallholder had not seen him.

Unfamiliar tastes enveloped Raffles's mouth as he wolfed down the meat with great pleasure. As he swallowed it, his mouth started to feel like it was on fire and his ears started to tingle. He quickly rushed over to the nearest puddle of water and slurped it up to try and ease the tingling.

Sunny let out a chuckle as he watched. 'You'll get used to it soon, Raffles.'

And with that, the monkey jumped onto Raffles's back and started to use his ears as reins to guide him away from the station.

Not far away was the entrance to an inviting green jungle of trees. The thick canopy was a very welcome shelter from the heat of the midday sun that was now beating down on them. As they marched through the trees, birds and crickets erupted into song. The noise was deafening. Large red flowers, some spikey and some soft, offered sweet nectar to birds and hiding places for bugs. The gentle sound of trickling water made a pleasant change to the frantic bustle they had just left behind. Raffles felt calmer and started to relax a little as they both ventured deeper into the undergrowth; Sunny began whistling a tune that Raffles had heard somewhere before.

Not far into the jungle, Raffles asked one of the many questions he was still longing to ask the monkey. 'How did you come to life?' he enquired. 'When I first saw you in Grandpa's shop you definitely weren't awake.'

Sunny smiled as he started to rummage through Raffles's fur, picking out little bugs that had hitchhiked a ride. 'Grandpa's shop is not all it seems, my friend. That shop has hidden wonders that open up worlds of unbelievable adventure. Haven't you ever wondered why the shop never gets cleaned and why it's so dusty?'

Raffles looked puzzled.

'The dust!' Sunny whispered. 'The dust is magic! The dust is the thing that can bring things to life if it's disturbed at the right time. I think your sneezes brought us here, Raffles.'

5

Am I Daydreaming?

Back in the shop Grandpa woke up suddenly, jolted by his arm falling off the armrest. Composing himself and wiping his mouth with his hanky, he heaved himself up off his chair and headed to the back of the shop where a small fridge and kettle stood.

Reaching for the bread bin, Grandpa sliced the end of a new crusty loaf and made a cheese and pickle sandwich. A strong mug of builder's tea with a dash of milk and a couple of cherry tomatoes accompanied this. Carefully, so as not to spill his tea, Grandpa ventured back to the front of the shop. It seemed eerily quiet and for a split second Grandpa had forgotten that Raffles was with him.

'Oh dear! I forgot a naughty bit of cheese for Raffles.' Grandpa tutted as he turned back to the kitchen to get it. As he did, he called cheerily for Raffles to come closer and collect his treat. 'Raffles. Raffles. Cheese!'

Nothing! No rush of fluff coming towards him. No bounding beast. No drooling dog. Nothing!

Grandpa felt a rise of panic fill his chest. He called for Raffles again and again as he put down his sandwich and went back through the shop corridors with haste. He listened carefully to try and hear if Raffles had got stuck somewhere.

It soon became clear that Raffles was nowhere to be found. Feeling full of despair, Grandpa reached the last corner of the shop where he came upon an outline of dust. The outline of the dust looked decidedly like Raffles. 'Oh! My word!' said Grandpa. 'I don't believe it. Could it be …?'

Memories and visions raced through Grandpa's mind as he reached for the nearest piece of furniture on which to lean. Carefully scouring the area for more evidence, another small scuffle of dust became apparent, this one looking very unfamiliar to Grandpa.

Grandpa rubbed his stubbly chin with concern. If that was Raffles's outline, and he had indeed gone where he himself hadn't been for years, who or what had made the small scatter of dust next to him? Grandpa pondered as he returned to his window seat and his sandwich.

After a moment of contemplation and a big mouthful of cheese, Grandpa settled back into his chair. A knowing smile slowly appeared on his face and there was even a noticeable twinkle in his once-sad eyes. Could it be that young Raffles had re-awoken the magic of the shop after all these years? A warm glow filled Grandpa's heart as he closed his eyes and waited expectantly for Raffles to return.

6

An Unexpected Meeting

Sunny the monkey and Raffles were resting in a small glade where the sunbeams sparkled through the trees. The bustle of the market now seemed very distant. Raffles lifted his head and stood up, giving his fur a good shake and making his ears fly around his head like a windmill.

The beauty of their surroundings was overwhelming. Everything in the rainforest was buzzing with life. Raffles put his nose to the ground and sniffed around, trying to find some familiar scents.

Suddenly, Sunny saw Raffles quicken his pace and dash off in the direction of a shadow. A butterfly was flitting about in the sunshine and Raffles was doing his best to keep up with it, darting this way and that, up and down, round and about and then back again. He did look funny. Sunny burst out laughing. He really liked his new little friend. A mad, jolly, dotty springer spaniel. How lucky he was to have been awoken by Raffles.

Sunny ran over and joined in the fun, his long arms and legs stretching up and waving about in the air. They both ended up in a tangle on the grass, enjoying each other's company. Sunny had forgotten what it was like to laugh so much that his tummy ached.

'We really should move on now,' he said, giggling, to the spinning dog. 'Not much further and you will see where we are going to stay for the night.'

The two companions continued to travel on together, with Sunny riding on Raffles's back. They felt refreshed after their stop and there was a new energy in their step. The trees began to thin and the sunshine flooded their path. They could hear water falling nearby and they could make out some steps in the undergrowth.

Raffles lifted his eyes upwards and saw the roof of a magnificent house before him.

Before venturing up to the house, Sunny and Raffles decided to wash at the edge of the nearby pool lying at the base of an impressive waterfall. They knew they needed to smarten themselves up before seeing anyone.

As they slid their paws and hot bodies into the sparkling blue water, the sensation of being covered by the refreshing liquid was like a dream. Tiredness receded and the cascading water seemed to fill them with even more energy.

Over mossy boulders and peppered pebbles they wandered, getting closer to the foot of the thunderous waterfall with every step. The air next to the torrent was refreshingly cool and little rainbows bounced across the top of the water, seeming to guide the way for them. Small fish tickled their toes and dazzling dragonflies skipped across the surface of the water. When the water got a little too deep for Sunny, he clambered onto

Raffles's back and enjoyed the rays of sunshine hitting his fur.

'Come on, Sunny, let's see what's behind the waterfall!' Raffles shouted excitedly as he bounded out of the water, causing the monkey to fall off his back. Before Sunny knew it, Raffles had disappeared behind the waterfall. Raffles was definitely starting to get a little braver with the new and unexpected situation he had found himself in. Sunny followed him in.

Behind the waterfall was a wet and rather chilly cave. The loud noise of the water tumbling down reminded Raffles of Mr Watson's tummy noises when he was feeling hungry.

His head dropped and his nose hoovered along the slimy floor until he reached a deep and stinking puddle that drew him in like a magnet. He plunged into the gooey brown liquid and delighted in the excitement of his find. Rolling onto his back with his paws in the air and his tummy exposed, he wriggled from side to side like a caterpillar.

Suddenly, through the curtain of water outside, Sunny saw the outline of something moving slowly towards the river and then crouching into a ball.

'Raffles! Raffles! There's something out there! The other side of the waterfall. Look!' the monkey demanded. They both stood still, one tail up and one tail down, trying to hear any clues. Mud was dripping from Raffles's coat. The booming of the waterfall was too loud and the outline of what they could see was too blurry.

Slowly but surely, they both crept out from behind the waterfall, first poking their noses out to see if they could smell what it was. Unfortunately, all the monkey could smell was the pongy dog standing beside him.

From a distance they could now see that the silhouette was a woman washing clothes by the side of the river. She wore a bright electric-blue sari with gold trim. A thin headscarf drifted delicately over her greying ebony hair which was lightly drawn into a long plait.

Raffles knew they wouldn't be able to sneak away without being noticed so he tried to hide behind a bush. However, Sunny was already approaching the newcomer at a brisk pace, so Raffles had no choice but to bravely follow him.

As they approached, she jumped up in surprise, almost falling into the water. She let out a small shriek and reached for her washing, which she had already laid out in the sunshine. Then she steadied herself, quickly gathered her things and stood, keeping a cautious eye on the two animals coming towards her.

As they came nearer to her, a look of realization and recognition dawned.

She had a soft, caring face. Tiny lines surrounded her bright hazel eyes and crossed her tanned skin. At the centre of her forehead was a small red jewel, which caught the sunlight and flashed like a beacon. Rosy cheeks and smiling lips, along with jet black eyelashes, made her the most beautiful person Raffles had ever seen.

Sunny stopped suddenly and rubbed his eyes. Her face was familiar and as he looked into her eyes, he was sure he felt a flutter in his heart. But this was not who he was expecting to see. This was no child but an elegant woman. Could this be his wonderful Tamira? Had so many years gone by?

'Sunny?' she questioned, slowly lowering herself back down to the ground. 'Is that you?'

'Yes, ma'am,' replied Sunny, now grinning from hairy ear to hairy ear. 'It is me, a little older, but it is me.'

'Oooh Sunny!' she exclaimed, 'I have been waiting for this moment, and for you, for what seems like my entire life!'

She and Sunny embraced each other with great warmth for a long time, before finally turning their attention to Raffles, who was now looking even more puzzled.

'Raffles, I'd like you to meet Tamira, my very best friend,' said Sunny as he encouraged Raffles to come closer.

'Hello, friend,' Raffles replied warmly, along with his normal greeting of a very fast tail-wag, a quick spin and a friendly bark. Any friend of Sunny's was going to be his friend too.

Tamira and Sunny now settled into an enthusiastic conversation and started to talk about the good old days. Raffles crept quietly up to them and settled down at their feet so he could hear more. He was quite grateful to get back into the dappled sunshine again to warm and dry his fur.

'Raffles, now is a good time for us to explain everything and tell you when the magic started,' the monkey said, as he perched himself on a smooth red rock, his tail gently dipping into the river.

Raffles sat upright resting on his front two paws, his head tilted slightly, keen to hear more. He was ready for a rest and loved stories, especially ones that helped make sense of things.

Both Tamira and Sunny excitedly took it in turns to tell Raffles the full story – a story so full of wonder that even Raffles could never have imagined it.

7

Tamira and Sunny's Story

'It was a long time ago, Raffles, when I was just four years old,' Tamira started her story. 'I lived with my parents in the old house at the top of these steps, where I live now.'

As Raffles and Sunny snuggled in more closely, the story unfolded.

'My mother was a seamstress who made the most elaborate saris for ladies to wear to weddings and festivals. The materials she used were luxurious and ornate, with lots of gold trimmings. Her patterns and designs, stitched to perfection for each special occasion, brought people from all over India to seek her skills. She was a very gentle and loving lady who was always very positive and happy. She had ebony-black hair, just like I did, and glistening eyes that would always look at people with such love and affection. She worked so hard, there were days when she had little time to spend with me, which made her very sad. I used to sit watching her for hours on end, but sometimes I became very bored and lonely.' Tamira swept her hair from in front of her eyes and straightened her headscarf.

'One day, my mother decided to make me something very special, to keep me company on the long days when she was busy working. She carefully handstitched the most wonderful, cheeky monkey, made with the finest and softest materials she had. She made him with her special love and took great care to fill him with soft stuffing. Amongst the stuffing she secretly sprinkled some magic dust that she had been given a long time ago.'

Sunny was looking a little embarrassed now as he looked down towards his torn and dirty tummy. Raffles shuffled a little closer to the monkey, noticing he was getting upset. Raffles was enjoying the story and kept his eyes focused on Tamira, whose voice was like a song to him. He did not yet realize that Sunny was the monkey in the story.

'When my mother gave me the monkey, she said this, "This monkey is made with love and will keep you company wherever you are and will always be a friend to you. Like the meaning of your name, Tamira, this little monkey is magic. He will bring happiness to your life and will take you on many adventures. But be gentle with him, he needs to be looked after in order to keep the magic alive."'

'I fell in love with him straight away,' Tamira said, as so many memories came flooding back to her.

She looked down at Sunny and gently stroked his once-fine golden-brown head and his faded pink ears. She touched his friendly face. The tips of her fingers followed every seam and detail that her mother had sewn into this little creature so long ago. The soft velvety material that used to tickle her nose when she cuddled him was now hard and worn-out and the shimmery ribbon and key that once sparkled was now drab and dull. But Tamira could still see he was magical, just as her mother had told her.

'From that day onward, I cared for you with all my heart and took you everywhere with me,' said Tamira, looking directly at Sunny. She touched him lightly and carefully pushed a small bulge of his stuffing back through the hole in his tummy.

'I need to fill you again with the magic you once had,' she smiled. 'You have come home to me for this purpose, my dear, sweet friend.' Sunny's eyes filled with happy tears as he listened to the soothing words being spoken to him.

'Oh my!' said Raffles, getting up abruptly onto his four paws, his tail standing straight and tall like a flagpole. 'You don't mean that Sunny is the same monkey that you had when you were little, do you? He can't be. How did he get so worn out? How did he get into Grandpa's shop? I still don't understand.'

The musical voice began speaking again. Raffles sat back down again and rested his head on Tamira's lap.

'Sunny went to England with my dearest friend, George,' she explained.

She began telling them about the day she met George, on her seventh birthday when she and her parents had joined in one of the many colourful street festivals. It was an extremely special day, one that Tamira would never forget.

George was at the festival with his parents. There were so many people in the streets, singing and dancing, that they all got squashed together. It was an instant friendship of kindred spirits, filled with fun and laughter.

'George, Sunny and I became the best of friends and each day after school we would enjoy playing outside in the jungle: swimming in streams, climbing rocks, swinging from trees and laughing until our tummies hurt. The days went so quickly and the adventures we went on were always magical. We called ourselves "The Three Adventurers".'

Raffles was in a daze now, trying to work out if he knew who George was. 'What happened to George, Sunny? Where is he now'

'Well, Raffles, one afternoon a few years later, whilst the heavens opened with rain and the skies boomed with thunder, we were told that George and his parents would be moving back to England where he was born. His dad's job in India had finished and George was due to start a new school,' Sunny replied.

'That's where I come from – maybe I could help you find George when I go home?' Raffles said excitedly, his tail wagging a little faster.

Tamira and Sunny glanced at each other and gave a small chuckle.

'You don't need to find him, Raffles, you already know him,' they both said together.

'Really?' Raffles pondered, 'how can that be?'

'Grandpa! George is Grandpa, Raffles,' said Sunny, bouncing up and down with glee.

Raffles was astonished. How could old grumpy Grandpa in his antique shop be happy-go-lucky young George?

'Yes, Raffles, it is true,' continued Tamira. 'George is older now, just like

Sunny and I. When George went back to England I gave him Sunny to make sure he never forgot me. I secretly put him into his rucksack before he left. I knew the magic would keep us together, however far apart we were.'

* * * * * * * * * * * *

On the plane back to England, George was feeling pretty low. Looking in his rucksack for something to eat he was surprised to find Sunny. A small black and white photograph fell out of his bag at the same time. He picked it up and gazed at it, deep in thought.

On the back of the photograph Tamira had written a note asking him to take care of Sunny and to remember her always. Looking at the photograph of 'The Three Adventurers', he noticed a sparkle that seemed to radiate from

Sunny. It must be a mark on the photo he thought. Examining the monkey sitting on his lap more closely, George noticed the vibrant green ribbon that someone had attached to Sunny with an elaborate brass key attached to the end of it. Tucked under the ribbon was a small envelope containing a letter sprinkled with dust.

Tamira must have put it there without him noticing.

George gently opened the letter that had been carefully folded four times. Here is what was written:

I am a monkey made from the heart
To keep you safe whilst we're apart.
If you get lost or need some direction
Then call on me to give you protection.
If adventure and love is what you require
with a sprinkle of dust, you will get your desire.
Into the future or back in the past,
All these adventures could have you aghast.
But care for me as your best friend
For if I break the magic will end.

8

The Ingredients of Magic

Back by the river, Raffles was now sitting even more upright and his big brown eyes hadn't blinked in what felt like twenty minutes. He was so engrossed in the story that Sunny and Tamira were telling him, he was a million miles away.

'Keep going,' Raffles pleaded, keen for the story not to end.

Sunny and Tamira looked at each other, admiring Raffles's enthusiasm and interest in their story.

'So, Grandpa brought Sunny back to England with him?' Raffles continued. 'What happened next? Why didn't Grandpa tell anyone about the magic? And how did you end up damaged, Sunny?' Questions continued to tumble out of Raffles's mouth.

'Well, Raffles,' the monkey started to explain, 'with a sprinkle of dust from the locket, Grandpa kept the magic going and, over the years, together we went on hundreds of adventures. To places near and far, all with the purpose of doing good deeds.'

Raffles's tummy started to flutter like a butterfly.

'Oh, the things we saw, Raffles, the amazing places and lands we visited and the weird and wonderful people we met,' the monkey continued. 'We had the time of our lives.'

Sunny suddenly looked sad and dropped his chin to his chest. 'That was until he lost Grandma, the love of his life, and started to forget the magic.'

'How can anyone forget magic?' Raffles questioned.

The monkey took a stick from the ground and started to draw a list in the small patch of sand that was next to him. 'There is a recipe to follow when you need this magic to happen, Raffles.

Happiness, a purpose, a sprinkle of dust and me.' This is what he wrote:

Magic ingredients
Happiness
Purpose
Magic dust
Monkey

'When Grandpa lost Grandma, he became really unhappy. He became very quiet and lonely and lost a lot of purpose to his life. At the same time, a few years ago, I slipped in between two cabinets and ripped my side,' said the monkey, examining the hole in his brown tummy. 'That was when I became lost in the antique shop for a very long time. Long enough for Grandpa to forget me and forget the magic.'

Raffles whiffled his nose into the monkey's side, nuzzled him close and planted a reassuring slobbery lick on his head.

'It was your sneezes in the shop that blew the dust in my face and reactivated the magic,' Sunny explained. 'Your energy brought happiness back into the shop after it had been lost for so long. You and I now have a job to do, Raffles.'

'We must get you fixed!' Raffles exclaimed, finally understanding enough to piece the puzzle together. 'But how?'

'I think that's where I come in,' Tamira said, as she pushed a wisp of hair behind her ear. 'My mother taught me how to be a seamstress just like her and I believe you have come here to be repaired, Sunny. When you are repaired, you must go straight back to George, make him happy and remind him of the magic that has been lost.'

'We have no time to lose,' she continued as she stood up and straightened her sari. 'Follow me to the house and we will start with some food; you must be so hungry. Also, you are both pretty grubby and in need of a good wash and a smarten-up.'

Raffles licked his lips and gave himself a shake, starting with his crispy ears and spreading down to his matted tail. A torrent of foul-smelling mud and water erupted from his coat and the smell of rotten apples wafted towards Tamira and Sunny, who were now running for cover.

'Phwoarrrr, Raffles, what have you been rolling in!' they both yelled, insisting he get back into the clear water of the river to clean himself. Raffles willingly obliged and bounced himself into the fresh water until his nose disappeared under the surface. As he came back up his little legs could be seen paddling madly, propelling him back towards the river bank. With a huge shower of water, Raffles darted out straight towards Tamira. This time the shake was much more pleasant.

'Wow, Raffles, I didn't realize you were brown and white! How lovely you look and how much better you smell,' she remarked.

Tamira gently scooped Sunny up into her arms and kissed him on his head as he clambered up onto her shoulder. He placed his arm around her neck and rested his head against her soft hair. The smell of her sweet perfume brought back so many long-forgotten memories for him.

The three companions started walking up the steps together, away from the river and towards Tamira's house.

The day was now cooling, with an orange tint to the sky. A warm breeze guided them up the steps and a thousand crickets were bursting into song, their loud chirping filling the jungle.

Over all this noise, Raffles could hear Sunny whistling the same tune he had heard earlier. Raffles finally knew where he had heard it before – it was the tune that Grandpa always whistled when he came to visit.

Another tiny tinkling noise was coming from up ahead. Raffles could now see that this was coming from Tamira's ankle, which was adorned with many exotic chains and beads. A small gold anklet stood out from the rest: the monkey charm in the middle was very clear to see.

As they reached the top of the steps and emerged into the late afternoon sun,

Raffles felt happy and content. He now finally understood why they were there and was glad he would soon be back to make Grandpa happy again.

But how on earth were they meant to get back?

9

Tamira's Home

At the top of the steps, the mossy path led into an enclosed garden, where the scent of the flowers was overwhelming. Raffles lifted his nose high into the air to catch the story being told by the breeze. A green lawn was being sprinkled with droplets of water from a hosepipe and the air felt fresh and clean. The grass was dotted by flowers dropped from large trees and colourful butterflies flitted around the garden like fairies at a tea party.

Tamira's house was a welcoming sight to Sunny and Raffles, whose tired legs were now starting to feel a little wobbly beneath them. The large peach-coloured building stood tall, with marble pillars and high ceilings. White bamboo shutters and arched doors with ornate patterns stood ajar, enticing the three of them in. Inside the hallway, large whirring fans cooled the air and made the comforting sound of home.

Three young children with tousled hair and sticky fingers came running excitedly to greet them. These were Tamira's grandchildren.

'I have a job for you three,' Tamira instructed them. 'I want you to help dry this scallywag of a dog, Raffles, with these towels and brush his coat. Only then will he be ready to sit with us for dinner. I have my own work cut out trying to repair this very loved and old monkey that I had when I was your age,' Tamira said, smiling gently. Sunny leant into her and rubbed his head along her fingers. He knew that the magic had brought him home for this very reason.

The children jumped up and down, giggling at the spectacle. Raffles was trying hard to understand everyone and tilted his head from side to side, listening intently. His tail had dried enough for the feathery plumes of hair to wave like a flag as he showed his happiness and excitement. The children took some towels and ran down into the garden with Raffles bounding after them.

Inside the house luxuriant green plants were dotted throughout, nestled into pots between the soft chairs and bamboo furniture scattered across the room.

'Now, my dear little Sunny, let me take you to my mother's old sewing room, where I can start to repair the results of all your adventures. You can tell me all about George and the adventures you went on. Did you forgive me for sending you to England? I missed you so much at first, but as I grew older, I knew that I had done the right thing giving you to George.'

Sunny smiled and cuddled up to Tamira, wrapping his arms around her neck as he used to. Tamira shut her eyes and suddenly she felt as though she was nine years old again.

Tamira carried him up the narrow staircase. At the top on the left was a doorway where rows of beads threaded together hung down from the door frame like the waterfall. They parted the beads and opened the door to a large, bright, airy room. Sunny remembered this room and could still imagine Tamira's mother sitting at her sewing machine in the window. This was where he was made. This was where he was created and given magical powers. This was where his life began.

'Yes, I needed to bring you to this room, Sunny, as this is where my mother stored all her materials. These are the ones she chose to make you special. If I can find the same ones that she used, I will be able to make you look as good as new,' Tamira said reassuringly.

Over the next hour, Tamira used her skill and ability to replicate her mother's stitching. Soft plush fabric was used to repair Sunny's broken ears. Stitch by stitch and thread by thread, his body gently healed and became whole again.

Outside in the garden, a commotion of excitement and giggling was coming from Tamira's grandchildren, who were now brushing Raffles's long and glossy coat, taming what had looked like a matted monster.

Tamira's gentle touch and delicate stitching caused Sunny no pain and with the sound of Raffles out in the garden having fun, he felt truly lucky. Lucky to have found himself back in India and back with his lovely friend Tamira, after all these years.

10

Transformation

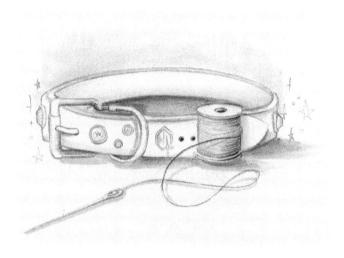

Once Sunny's tummy was repaired and he was tenderly cleaned, he was gently placed onto the window ledge where he continued to watch Tamira's magic unfold.

She turned her attention to replacing the grubby frayed ribbon and polishing the key. The ribbon was then gently placed over the monkey's head.

Once Tamira had finished, Sunny jumped over to the tall mirror which stood near the door. He couldn't believe his eyes! Had he always been this good-looking and had he always looked so smart? His fur stood to attention and looked soft and fluffy and his tummy, despite having a small scar, looked back to normal. The emerald-green ribbon and shiny key looked like a medallion. He felt truly complete and started to shed a little tear.

'Wowee, Tamira, thank you so much!' he exclaimed, continuing to admire his good looks in the mirror. 'You have done such a good job. I look young again!'

Tamira smiled proudly at the monkey and then set to work on her next project.

Time was running out and she had to be quick.

Sunny ran his fingers along his neatly stitched scar and for a moment he forgot where he was, whilst memories flooded back to him. Happy ones, sad ones, exciting ones and scary ones. Memories that made him feel alive again and memories that he had forgotten for a long time.

Suddenly, a demanding bark from a hungry Raffles was heard from downstairs.

'Come on, Sunny, let's go and get some food.' Tamira got to her feet, setting down her tools and picking up something shiny.

He bounced back to reality and went jumping down the stairs with Tamira close behind.

At the bottom of the stairs stood a glorious-looking furry beast. A majestic brown and white dog standing tall and proud with an extremely silky white chest. His long hairy ears, which looked neatly crimped, blew gently in the breeze and his bright eyes looked up eagerly towards the monkey.

Similarly, what Raffles saw from the bottom of the stairs was not the broken and dusty Sunny that he knew but a royal-looking monkey showered in love and care.

They both stopped and stood still for a moment, taking in each other's new looks. How handsome they both looked!

'Wow, Sunny, you look amazing, and so different!' Raffles exclaimed as the monkey came bounding down the stairs towards him.

'You don't look too bad yourself, my friend,' the monkey said, gently nuzzling into Raffles's ear, which now smelt of strawberries. 'Definitely a lot more like a dog rather than a mud monster,' and they giggled.

Admiring the splendour of Sunny's newly repaired tummy, Raffles was unaware of Tamira coming up to him and placing something around his neck. He looked up towards Tamira, who was now crouching down next to them both, beaming with pride.

'You look wonderful, Raffles, but you needed a little something extra to wear, something as handsome and as special as you are,' she said. 'Something that binds you to India and to each other,' she added, tickling them both under their chins and holding a hand-held mirror in front of them both.

An elegant handmade white collar covered with jewels and beading had been placed around the scruff of Raffles's neck. It fitted perfectly.

Raffles suddenly felt a warmth inside him that went all the way from his hairy toes up to his wet brown nose. It was a tingly warmth that made him feel as if he was in a bubble of love, protection and overwhelming comfort.

'I've never worn anything as beautiful as this, it is amazing. Is this really for me?' Raffles exclaimed.

'You deserve it, Raffles,' Tamira replied. 'Your happiness and free-spirited attitude brought Sunny back to me, which means that now the magic can continue for many years to come. If it hadn't been for you, it could have been lost forever.'

Drawn together like a big magnet, Raffles, Sunny and Tamira scooped each other up and squeezed each other as tight as they could, pleased that Raffles now smelt nice.

Had Raffles really only met them both this morning?

'Right, my two little friends, you must both be starving!' Tamira said, giving them a quick tweak on their ears. They really did both look amazing and she felt so proud of her handiwork.

11

A Wonderful Feast

Raffles and Sunny followed Tamira into the next room and were greeted by the sight of Tamira's whole family sitting on big bright floor cushions dotted around a low wooden table.

Dishes of big fat juicy fruits, oven-baked pies, spicy-smelling curries, luscious lentils, towering flatbreads, bright salads and succulent meats covered the table. The smells that filled the air were some of the best Raffles had ever smelt and he couldn't help but start to dribble.

'Find a cushion, you two, and help yourself, there is plenty to go round.'

Tamira's family were chatting and laughing with excitement as the guests entered the room and took their places, each on a plump cushion.

With subtle guidance from Sunny to make sure he avoided the extra-spicy foods, Raffles felt as if he were in a dream. Every spice and flavour that erupted on his tongue caused a tingle and some flavours even seemed to tickle the inside of his ears.

They ate until their tummies were full to the brim, and chatted until their jaws hurt and a cloud of sleepiness enveloped them both.

Raffles stood up and stretched his tired legs out in front of him, whilst giving a very big yawn. His stretch extended from his head to the tip of his tail with little quivery movements, relaxing his weary body.

He wandered over to a small rug that was placed near the door. He pawed it a few times before circling his body round, to make sure he found the comfiest position to rest himself in. He flopped to the floor with a big sigh and started to nestle his head into the folds of the rug. His gentle spaniel eyes were now very droopy with sleep.

Seeing how comfortable Raffles looked on the rug, Sunny decided to follow him over, tail dragging on the floor. He settled himself down, cuddling into Raffles's neck, lifting his ear and placing it over his belly like a blanket.

With a sad smile on her face, Tamira excused herself from the table and quietly walked over to the sleepy pair.

'My dear little friends, your busy day is nearly over. Soon you will be back where you belong and your purpose will be fulfilled,' she said, as she gently tucked a piece of paper under the ribbon on Sunny's tummy.

'I have loved every moment with you two, and I would love for you to stay, but you must go back to George now; he needs your sweet kindness and energy to bring back his memories and brighten his life again.'

She softly placed the scarf from her head over the two of them, ran her fingers through their fur and placed a kiss on each forehead.

In the comfort of their surroundings, content and happy, Raffles and Sunny quickly drifted off into a deep sleep.

'Safe travels, my friends. Please don't forget me.' A small tear ran down her rosy cheek as she clipped a dainty locket, full of magic dust, next to the key on the ribbon.

12

Grandpa's Memory Box

Over the hedge, under the fence, around the molehills and through the long grass ran Raffles in pursuit of a rabbit, his legs moving faster and faster as he let out small whimpers. Suddenly a bell rang out, stopping Raffles in his tracks …

'I'll have that polished up and ready for you to collect tomorrow, Mrs James,' Grandpa explained as the door to the antique shop closed with a ding of the bell.

Raffles woke up.

It took a few minutes to realize where he was. Had it all been a dream? Where was he now?

Before he knew it, Grandpa was rushing over to him, letting out a delighted laugh and bombarding him with affection. 'How glad I am to see you back here, Raffles. I was starting to get a little worried you wouldn't be back in time for pickup. I wonder where you got to by yourself?'

Raffles gazed up towards Grandpa, wanting to tell him all about his incredible dream. However could he explain? He stood up and gave an energetic shake and followed Grandpa over to the chair in the window.

'Well, well, what on earth is round your neck, Raffles?' Grandpa remarked, admiring his sparkly collar. 'You are looking so smart and handsome.'

Raffles's ears pricked up as he suddenly realized that perhaps his day had not all been a dream. Nose to the floor, he ventured back over to where he had awoken.

There before him was his friend Sunny. Beaming with pleasure, Raffles pressed his nose into the monkey's side, pleased to know his friend was indeed real. This time though, the monkey remained still and quiet, just as Raffles had originally found him. The difference was that he was now repaired and looked like new.

A mix of emotions ran through Raffles's mind. He lovingly picked Sunny up with his soft mouth and took him over to Grandpa, placing Sunny onto his lap.

Grandpa picked up the object that had been placed on his knee, held it up in front of his eyes, and looked at it in deep contemplation. Raffles watched as Grandpa's expression changed as soon as he realized what he was looking at. His eyes started to fill with tears and a broad smile stretched across his face.

'Well, I never! My trusted travelling companion. Where did you find him, Raffles? I had forgotten all about him,' Grandpa said sadly with a lump in his throat. He looked deeply into Sunny's big familiar brown eyes and held him up against his own wet cheek.

'Sunny, my friend, how splendid you look! I thought I had lost you, just like Grandma. I thought any magic in my life had gone forever.' He gently wept into his hanky.

Sitting beside Grandpa, Raffles lifted his front paw and touched Grandpa's leg to comfort him.

'I'm alright, Raffles, just a bit emotional,' Grandpa said, patting Raffles on the head.

Yet again, Raffles pawed at Grandpa's leg and this time pushed Sunny closer, encouraging Grandpa to take a closer look.

Grandpa, still a little blubbery, took the hint from Raffles and started to examine Sunny in more detail. He noticed the ribbon and ran his big fingers along it until he reached the locket and a shiny brass key attached. A small note was tucked under the ribbon, just like it had been all those many years ago.

Delicately unfolding the piece of paper with his large hands, Grandpa went on to read the note aloud.

My dearest George,

Who would have thought that all these years later, a happy-go-lucky dog would bring Sunny back to me in India? I have managed to repair him and the magic of our childhood has now been restored. He comes with my love, a new locket of dust and the key to your memory box. We have both grown old and forgetful and need to keep this magic and adventure in our lives. Raffles and Sunny will bring you great joy. Enjoy your adventures.

Your forever friend Tamira x

With shaky hands, Grandpa refolded the note and placed it into his pocket. He couldn't quite believe that his childhood friend had contacted him after all these years and restored the magic that he had forgotten for so long.

Memories raced through his mind. He could hear Tamira's sweet laughter, feel the heat of the jungle, hear the noise of the crickets and the rush of the waterfall as he was transported back to being ten years old again.

Raffles suddenly let out an insistent bark, bringing Grandpa back from his thoughts.

'So, Raffles! Your first adventure with Sunny was to see Tamira in India where it all began. How clever of you to have awoken the magic that was so important in my life. Thank you so much, Raffles, my lovely boy.'

Turning his attention back to the brass key in his hand and twiddling it between his fingers he tried to remember what it could possibly open.

As Grandpa rifled through his thoughts and memories, Raffles started tugging at the Indian rug that was covering the big box he had sat on that morning. Suddenly Grandpa was eagerly pulling the rug off with him until it fell to the floor with a puff of dust.

There in front of them was the forgotten memory box – a dark wooden chest with busy images carved into it, each one telling a story. Without hesitation, Grandpa used the key to open the chest and lifted the lid.

Raffles poked his nose over the top of the chest so he could get a closer look at what was inside. The smell of the wood reminded him of Tamira's house.

Old papers, glossy photographs and old trinkets were piled high in the box, each one put there by Grandpa after one of his adventures. Grandpa started to pick up single objects to admire, each one reminding him of a special memory. He started to talk excitedly about places and people that Raffles had never heard of. His face lit up with joy and the twinkle in his eyes had finally returned.

To Raffles this box looked like a dusty extension of the antique shop but to Grandpa it was like a hundred birthdays in one. Never had Raffles seen Grandpa so full of energy and excitement.

'Here you go, Raffles, you'll recognize this photo,' Grandpa said as he lifted a black and white photograph from the box.

In the photograph Raffles recognized Tamira and Sunny sitting by the river where he had been that day. Next to them was a young boy who resembled a younger and less hairy Grandpa. The sparkle that surrounded Sunny could clearly be seen in the photo.

At that moment the clocks in the antique shop started chiming four o'clock.

'Goodness, Raffles, is that the time? We must put this all away quickly. You will be collected soon and no one else must find out our secret. I will put your travelling collar into my box for safe keeping until next time.'

Grandpa placed the locket of dust and the collar safely into the chest before closing the lid and locking it. Placing the rug back over the chest and the key back around Sunny's shoulders. Grandpa rested the monkey beside his chair for safety. 'Rest there, my little adventurer,' Grandpa reassured him.

'Ding!' went the bell above the door as Eva walked into the shop. 'Hello Dad, hello Raffles. How has your day been? Not too boring, I hope?' she asked.

Raffles and Grandpa looked at each other with knowing smiles. 'Oh, it's been wonderful,' replied Grandpa enthusiastically.

Much to the surprise of Eva, not only did Raffles look extremely smart and fluffy, Grandpa was also looking very lively and bright. He had a spring in his step as he came to the door to greet her and Freddie.

'Brilliant, I'm glad he behaved himself. I did worry Raffles would be too much for you. Are you happy to have him again tomorrow?'

'Of course,' Grandpa replied, 'more than happy. Raffles and I have a lot to be getting on with.'

Eva looked puzzled but relieved at his answer.

Grandpa trotted over to Raffles and put his lead on, ruffling his ears at the same time. 'Thank you for today, lad,' he whispered. 'Sunny, you and I will have to go somewhere special tomorrow. I want to come with you next time.'

'Right, Dad, must dash; I need to go and collect the sausages from the butcher. Thanks again for all your help. I'll see you in the morning.'

Grandpa passed the lead over to Eva and whistled his way off to the kitchen at the back of the shop, saying goodbye as he went. He didn't even seem to need his walking stick.

Eva pulled the shop door shut, chuffed to see how happy her dad was. 'Raffles, you and Grandpa seem to make a great team. I have no idea how you have cheered him up so much, but I love you for it. Let's go and get the sausages, shall we?'

Raffles licked his lips. What a day it had been. His heart felt warm and fuzzy. He and Sunny had fulfilled their purpose and had brought happiness back into Grandpa's life.

He wondered what excitement tomorrow would bring for 'The Three New Adventurers'.

But first ... sausages for tea!!

Be Kind.

Be Brave.

Be more Raffles.

9 781839 757204